Coconut Jack

EGMONT

We bring stories to life

First published in Great Britain 2008
by Egmont UK Ltd.
239 Kensington High Street, London W8 6SA
Text copyright © Jill Lewis 2008
Illustrations copyright © Erica Jane-Waters 2008
The author and illustrator have asserted their moral rights.
ISBN 978 1 4052 4132 8
10 9 8 7 6 5 4 3 2 1
A CIP catalogue record for this title is available from the British Library.
Printed in Singapore.

Coconut Jack

Written by

Illustrated by

Jill Lewis Erica-Jane Waters

Blue Bananas

This is the homework Year One got.

Make something special for our jungle display.

Bring it in to school on Monday.

This is the class –
excited and keen
to get on with making
a jungle scene.

With lots of ideas
whizzing about,
everyone's chatting
as they hurry out.

Look at this drawing by
Declan and Peter.
Can you guess what
it is? A giant
anteater!

They'll make
it with clay,
put marks on the
back, bake it for ages
and then paint it black.

6

Angela's making a large jungle hut.

She's planning the roof,

now the blinds

are shut . . .

I've had a great idea!

This is a rainforest millipede

and

walking

beneath it are Ben

and Sayeed.

This is Ricky

covered in glue.

Enjoying himself,

he's making bamboo.

And this is Harry and twin sister Heather. They've made a big bird, with one tail feather.

I'm stuck!

They used paper maché
and painted the
wings, then stuck
on a beak and a few
other things.

And this is
a new girl.

Her name
is Lin May.
She only arrived
the other day.

She can turn rubbish

and bits of old tat

into

something

which looks

as gorgeous

as **THAT!**

And this is
what others in
Year One
are doing.

Spending
time on
their
homework,

14

cutting

and gluing.

Well, all except

one boy . . .

and his

name is Jack.

He walked out of school and never looked back.

Yippee!

There's so much to do and so little time. There's a football to kick and a big tree to climb.

16

And this is what Jack said
to Mum, Dad
and Gran.

'There's still
time for homework,
cos I've got a plan.'

Done it! He went to his room for two minutes flat, then came back downstairs

announcing, 'That's that!' Back into the garden he hurried to play.

18

Mum looked at the others.

'What did he say?!
He's not finished
already, that
can't be so!'

That was fast!

She went to Jack's room, saw
the modelling dough and . . .

19

21

This is the tree, two metres tall,
made out of cardboard by
Dad in the hall,

That's better!

to hold up the
coconut Jack made.

This is the vine,

knitted in twine,

made by Jack's grandma

in double quick time,

that swings from the tree

(two metres tall),

made out of cardboard

by Dad in the hall . . .

that holds up

the coconut

Jack made.

This is the snake so heavy
and green, made from Mum's scarf
on her sewing machine,

which winds

round the vine

that swings

from the tree . . .

that holds up the

coconut Jack made.

This is

Fred's parrot,

red, blue and green,

perched on the snake,

the longest you've

seen,

which winds

round the vine

that swings from

the tree . . .

26

that holds up the

coconut Jack made.

27

This is the 'tiger',

donated by Fred

(no, it's not real but

a soft toy instead).

It lies in the branches

right next to the snake.

Everything starts to

wobble and shake.

28

And this is

the vine

that swings

from the

tree . . . that holds up the

coconut Jack

made.

This is Jack's family,

all looking smug

What a display!

but Jack's not bothered.

He says, with a shrug: 'I liked

my coconut, thanks all the same.'

And he goes off

to finish his

football game.

This is Monday and Harry and Heather. Both want to carry the bird with the feather. So the au pair's decided she'll take it instead

Careful!

and is having to hold it high over her head.

And this is Lin May

and Rick's coming too,

Hello, Rick!

holding his sticks
of homemade bamboo.

33

And this is Jack's journey to school in the car.

It's just as well it's not far . . .

And this is Jack's family

unloading it all

Mind the vine!

and taking it carefully into the hall.

They set it up
beautifully;
leaving one
space in a
branch
of the tree,
the perfect
place.

Just right for

the coconut

Jack made!

Here's the display on the

walls and the floor.

But a water pipe's burst in

the corridor.

And this is the plumber

who's mending the leak.

He's been trying to fix it

for nearly a week.

The water is flooding into the hall.

It's up to Jack's knees

in no time at all.

This is the tiger

who fancies a swim,

joined by Jack's

classmates

who dive after him.

And this is the parrot

floating nearby.

The head teacher's shouting

(but no one

knows why),

so she grabs the

snake to make a lasso

but the effort of spinning it

breaks it in two.

And this is Lin May, Rick and the twins

Whee!

bobbing about in their 'boats' made from bins. They hurtle past Dad, who's trying to net some of his woodwork but it's getting wet.

This is the water
up to Mum's
thighs.
The plumber
feels guilty:

'I'm so sorry, guys . . .'

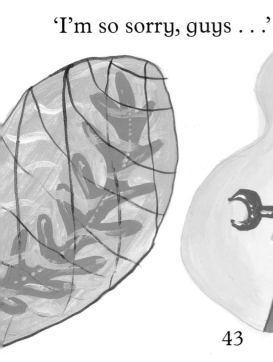

And look at the vine,

unravelling fast,

catching on everything

as it floats past.

Angela's hut,

the bird

with the feather

and Rick's bamboo

all sink together.

Now all is a tangle,

a knot and a noise,

so nobody notices one

group of boys climbing the

tree . . . till they hear the

crash as it hits the water

with one mighty

SPLASH!

And everything's ruined

and soggy and wet,

except for one thing.

You've guessed it, I bet,

and that is . . .

. . . the **COCONUT** Jack made!!!